# Hello Kitty®

## Guide to Life

First published in the UK by HarperCollins Children's Books in 2009
3 5 7 9 10 8 6 4 2
ISBN: 978-0-00-732622-8

A CIP catalogue record for this title is available from the British Library.
No part of this publication may be reproduced, stored in a retrieval system or
transmitted in any form or by any means, electronic, mechanical, photocopying,
recording or otherwise, without the prior permission of HarperCollins
Publishers Ltd, 77-85 Fulham Palace Road, Hammersmith, London W6 8JB.
www.harpercollins.co.uk
Printed and bound in China

# Hello Kitty®

# Guide to Life

HarperCollins *Children's Books*

# Welcome
## to Hello Kitty's Guide to Life!

There were so many things I wanted to share with you, so I've tried to pack in as much information on how to make your life as fun and fashionable as possible.

You can find all of my hints on how to get your own look, top tips on personalising your room and some suggestions on how to have fun with your friends. Once you've done all of that, you can read my guides to some of my favourite cities and decide which one you want to visit first, cook up a couple of my favourite recipes and then pick a new hobby to take up once you've finished reading! There are so many exciting things to do and try, I think there's something for everyone.

I hope this book makes you smile!
Love,

*Hello Kitty*
xx

# Contents

Hello Kitty®

Pretty Hello Kitty

# Basic skincare

 **It's super important to take care of your skin. Here are my top five tips:**

✶ Cleanse every morning and evening! Use a gentle cleanser so you don't strip your skin. Harsh astringent cleansers will make your skin greasier, not cleaner.

✶ Always moisturise after you cleanse. Even young skin needs a light moisturiser to keep it looking its best.

✶ Never go outside without an SPF. The sun can damage your skin even when it's cloudy.

✶ Get lots of beauty sleep. Skin repairs itself while you're sleeping - that's why you always wake up with a glow!

✶ Try and drink five glasses of water a day and eat lots of vegetables. Whatever you put in your body will show up on your skin...

**Once a week, it's a good idea to pamper your skin with a face mask. Here are a couple of masks you can make yourself at home.**

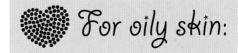 For oily skin:

**Ingredients:**
✶ 1 banana, preferably ripe (you can keep ripe bananas in the freezer. Let it thaw before using)
✶ 1 tbsp honey
✶ An orange or a lemon

**Preparation:**
Mix the banana and honey together. Add a few drops of juice from an orange or a lemon. Apply to face for 15 minutes then rinse.

## ❤ For dry skin:

**Ingredients:**

- ★ 1 egg yolk
- ★ 1tsp runny honey
- ★ 1tsp olive oil
- ★ Vitamin E oil (optional)

**Preparation:**

Mix the egg yolk, honey and olive oil and some vitamin E oil if you have it. Smooth on and leave for 15 minutes. Rinse in lukewarm water and pat dry. If your skin is a bit dry you can put a dab or two of olive oil, or any other light oil, on your moist skin after washing and your face is set without the ££ some people spend for the same look.

# Basic make-up

Wearing too much make-up is like wearing a mask - no one can see the real you! Everyone looks their best when their natural beauty shines through.

2. You might want to add a touch of blusher on to the apples of your cheeks if you're feeling pale. Try a peachy-pink shade and go lightly! It's always easier to add more blusher than to take it away.

1. Even out your skin tone with a light tinted moisturiser, a touch of powder on your chin and nose if you're shiny and concealer on any blemishes you want to cover up.

3. For an everyday eye, try a shimmery taupe or an icy lilac, framed with a coat of brown-black mascara. Perfectly framed peepers every time!

4. Lip balm is a must to keep your pout soft and protected. Try and use one with an SPF when you're out and about.

5. A rosy pink lipstick or gloss is perfect to finish your look.

# Basic hair

It's important to look after your hair to keep it shiny and healthy - think about how many times a week you wash it, blow dry it, brush it, tie it - wouldn't you be exhausted? Time for a little TLC for your tresses.

1. When you wash your hair, make sure it is soaked through before you shampoo and try not to get it all knotted up. Be as gentle as possible!
2. Gently squeeze the excess water out of your hair before you condition and then run the conditioner through the ends. Leave it on for a minute or two while you shower.
3. Don't ever rub your hair with a towel or brush it when it's wet! Hair is extra fragile when it's wet so blot with a towel and then tackle tangles with a wide-toothed comb.
4. Try to let your hair dry naturally a couple of times a week. Blow drying too often can make it weak and dull.
5. To help repair your hair, use a deep conditioner once a week. Try making your own with this easy recipe!

**Ingredients:**
* avocado
* 1 small jar real mayonnaise

**Preparation:**
Mash up the avocado and mix well with the mayonnaise to create a mint green coloured paste. Apply to damp hair and leave for 20 minutes. Rinse out thoroughly.

# Fun make-up

Having fun with make-up is a great way to express your personality and try out new looks. These suggestions are perfect for parties!

## Eye-eye!

Eye colour doesn't always have to be brown or grey. Try a bright jade green or cobalt blue, keeping the colour close to your lashline and framing with a flick of black mascara.

## Metallics

A fashion trend that keeps coming back is metallic make-up. To give this futuristic look a go, try a metallic eye shadow all over your lid, up to the crease. Go with silver if you're fair-skinned or gold if your skin has warmer tones.

## Flashy lashes

If you don't want to try too bright a colour on your lids, how about a flash of coloured mascara? A bright blue or purple applied to the tips of your lashes can be a fun look and makes the whites of your eyes look brighter!

## Pretty pout

Another good way to try new colours is to pick up some inexpensive lip glosses. If you really love a colour but are worried it won't work for you, lip glosses are usually sheerer than lipsticks. Or try mixing a lipstick with a little clear lip balm to get a softer version of that colour.

## Rainbow bright

The most risk free way to try new colours is on your nails. Keep them short and rounded and just pick whatever colour takes your fancy! Always use a basecoat to prevent the colour from staining.

# Basic need to know

It's not easy being a fashion icon! There's only one way to find out what style works for you - try as many out as you can until you find something that feels comfortable.

1. Always take something into the changing room that you hate and see what it looks like on. You might surprise yourself!

Everyone needs at least one good pair of jeans. Try a dark blue bootcut pair that you can dress up with heels and dress down with flats.

3. A perfect party dress is a must! As well as being super pretty, it should be comfortable enough to eat and dance in - although not at the same time!

A plain white T-shirt can work with a million outfits. Add it to your jeans and flats for simple chic. Swap out the flats for heels and add some jewellery for the perfect going out look!

When you're buying a coat, you need to make sure it goes with everything else in your wardrobe. It should be really comfortable, so make sure you move around a lot when you're trying it on. A neutral colour like black, navy or grey is usually best as they go with all the crazy colours you might wear underneath!

# Dressing up

**Getting dressed up for a party can be fun but sometimes scary. Follow these simple tips to make it easy, stylish and enjoyable!**

1.

Find out as much as you can about the event you're attending. Is it a dinner? A dance? A barbecue? If you're still not sure what to wear, ask someone who is also attending what they're planning to wear.

2.

The night or weekend before the party, try on your outfit and shoes and test your make-up just to make sure you're comfortable with everything. Always, always check that there is room for everything you need in your handbag.

3.

If you're still not sure what to wear, go with something you love. It's always better to be underdressed than overdressed!

4.

To refresh an old favourite, add some new accessories, like a pretty necklace or a brooch or even just a sparkly lip gloss. Or you could channel a certain Hello Kitty and add a big red bow to your hair...

5.

Leave plenty of time to get ready, there's nothing worse than being rushed. If you have friends going to the same party, why not get ready together?

# Get crafty!

Sometimes it's just impossible to find exactly what you want to wear and so you'll just have to make it yourself! Always check with your mama or papa before you start crafting and be very careful if you're planning on using scissors or sewing.

## One white T-shirt – three ways!

1. Take some pink lace or ribbon and glue it carefully around the edge of the T-shirt at the hem, the neckline and around the sleeves.

2. Take a plain white T-shirt and jazz it up with some fabric paints. You can draw any design you like, in any colour. Make sure you practise your design on some paper before you start on the T-shirt.

3. Pick some pretty buttons and sew or glue them on to the front of the T-shirt. They don't have to match and the sparklier, the better!

## Some other easy craft ideas...

When you're growing out of your jeans, cut them up into shorts! If you're feeling extra crafty, you could open up the seam and sew the ends together to make a cute skirt. Don't worry about hemming, the frayed edges are all part of the look.

Try turning a too long A-line skirt into a cool puffball. Carefully open up the seam in the hem and thread a piece of elastic all the way through. Once you get all the way round, make one or two stitches to fix the elastic together and even out your new puffball hem.

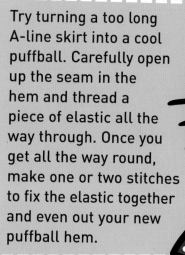

# Hello Kitty's favourite styles

# LONDON

London is home to lots of lovely things, Buckingham Palace, Big Ben and Hello Kitty!

## Places to visit:

**Buckingham Palace –** This is where the Queen lives. If the flag is raised outside, then she's at home!

**The London Eye –** You can see all of London from the top of this big wheel.

**The Natural History Museum –** So much to see and do, and there's an ice rink outside in winter.

## Places to eat:

**Fryer's Delight -** London's most delicious fish & chips.
**The Ritz -** Go for the most famous afternoon tea in the world!
**Konditor & Cook -** Make sure you stop by for a piece of Curly Whirly cake.

## Places to shop:

**Selfridges -** This famous department store is full of designer trinkets and Hello Kitty goodies!
**Hamley's -** There is always so much to see at Hamley's, it's like a giant playground!
**TopShop -** The Oxford Circus branch of TopShop is famous for attracting lots of fashionistas and celebs.

# NEW YORK

## The Big Apple

is one of the most exciting cities in the world. There's so much to see and do, make sure you plan ahead. It is the city that never sleeps after all!

## Places to visit:

**The Statue of Liberty:** Given as a gift to the USA from the people of France, Lady Liberty is 151 feet and one inch tall. The tablet she carries shows the date of the Declaration of Independence.

**The Empire State Building:** This famous building has appeared in hundreds of films and TV shows. Take the elevator to the top for amazing views of New York City!

**Central Park:** Central Park covers 843 acres in the middle of the city! New York's residents cycle, ride horses and in winter, even ice skate in the park.

I ♥ NY

N.Y.C. TAXI
K T

## Places to eat:

**Magnolia Bakery:** Mmm, these are the best cupcakes ever! And chocolate brownies and cookies and red velvet cake and...

**Katz's Deli:** Try the pastrami on rye bread sandwich in this famous old New York deli, it's delicious.

**Lombardi's Pizza:** For real, traditional Italian-American pizza, try Lombardi's in SoHo, yum. Make sure you have lots of room, these pizzas are huge!

## Places to shop:

**Tiffany & Co:** Tiffany's is home to New York's most fabulous, super pretty, super sparkly jewellery.

**Sanrio Store Times Square:** My favourite store in all of New York!

**Bloomingdales:** This store is shopper's heaven. Make sure you get one of their famous Little Brown Bags before you leave.

**Dylan's Candy Store:** Run by famous fashion designer Ralph Lauren's daughter, Dylan, you'll find all kinds of delicious treats in this fun and friendly candy store.

# PARIS

Ooh la la, Paris is one of the most beautiful cities in the world. Make sure you leave lots of time to wander around its beautiful streets and see absolutely everything there is to see.

Beauté

## Places to visit:

**The Eiffel Tower:** Join the 200,000,000 people that have already visited the Eiffel Tower for a beautiful view of Paris.

**Notre Dame:** Notre Dame is the most famous cathedral in Paris. See if you can spot its famous hunchback hiding behind the gargoyles!

**The River Seine:** I love taking a Bateaux-Mouche boat ride up the river to see all of Paris' beautiful buildings and landmarks on a sunny day.

## Places to eat:

**Centre Pompidou:** Pick any of the cafés by the Centre Pompidou and order a Chocolat Chaud and crepe outside the modern art museum that is practically a work of art itself!

**Ladurée:** Most famous for their double decker macaroons, Ladurée has been serving tea to stylish Parisians since 1862.

**Le Pick-Clops:** Head to this stylish café in the Marais district and watch the world go by.

## Places to shop:

**Collette:** If you're looking for everything that is stylish and cutting edge in the world of fashion, make sure you visit Collette.

**Chanel:** Paris is the fashion capital of the world and the biggest and best of all the fashion houses is Chanel. No trip to Paris would be complete without visiting the original boutique.

**Antoine & Lili:** For more fun and cute gifts, shoes and dresses, try Antoine & Lili. The shop is even painted pink!

# TOKYO

Konichiwa! **Tokyo** is home to some of the coolest styles in the world. Save up for some super shopping!

## Places to visit:

**Imperial Palace:** You can't actually go inside the Imperial Palace as it is home to the Emperor of Japan but you can explore the pretty Kokyo Gaien outside.

**Kiyosumi gardens:** These are some of the most famous gardens in all of Japan. Make sure you say hello to all the colourful carp and turtles in the ponds!

**Tokyo Tower:** Pop to the top of the Tokyo Tower for amazing views of the city. On a clear day, you can even see Mount Fuji.

## Places to eat:

**Daiwa Sushi:** Find Tokyo's best sushi inside the Tsukiji fish market. It's delicious!

**Tonki:** One of the biggest restaurants in Japan and famous for its Tonkatsu, or deep fried pork.

**Noodle bars:** Try some noodles from a street vendor. I think udon are the yummiest.

## Places to shop:

**Harajuku:** The bright and funky young residents of this famous district have inspired so many fashionistas, like Katy Perry and Gwen Stefani. Make sure you've got your camera!

**Shibuya 109 Building:** Full of quirky and cool stores, this is where Tokyo's hipsters come to shop.

**Ameyoko Plaza Food and Clothes Market:** This is a one stop shopping area for everything you could need and is great for souvenirs.

All About You

# Make a list and make it happen

I love making lists! Lists can help you keep yourself organised and help you plan for things you really want. Choose a special notebook then write down all the things that you want to happen in your life.

You might find it helps to have different lists, one for short term goals, one for things you want to get done this month and one for things you want to achieve in the longer term, like your dreams and ambitions.

## Things to do this week

* Tidy my room
* Get a haircut
* Finish my art project

## Things to do this month

* Put all my photos in albums
* Wardrobe sort out
* Save new cds on my computer

Hello Kitty®

# Things to do!

- ★ Learn to play guitar
- ★ Become a fashion designer
- ★ Visit New York

Once you've written your lists, keep the notebook with you or hidden away in a special place. Remember to cross off everything on your list once you've achieved it and add new things when you think of them. Just having the lists will keep these things in your mind and you'll be much more likely to make them happen.

# Don't worry, be happy!

When you're in a bad mood, it's really easy to sit alone and sulk but where's the fun in that? Instead, try thinking of something fun to do to brighten your mood. Here are some ideas.

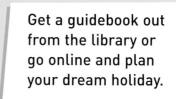

Get a guidebook out from the library or go online and plan your dream holiday.

Wrap up warm and go for a walk in your nearest park.

Play with your pet. If you don't have a pet, give your favourite stuffed animal a cuddle.

Bake something -
try the delicious
**chocolate chip cookie
recipe** on **page 76**.

Play your favourite
song over and over
and sing it out loud.

Watch your favourite movie
from when you were
younger and sing or act
along with every word.

# Study skills

**Studying doesn't have to be a chore! Learning something new can be exciting and help you make lots of interesting new friends. Here are my top tips on how to make study time a fun time.**

**1.** Whether you're studying for a project, an exam or something fun like a new language or a musical instrument, make sure you always have enough time. It's too stressful to leave things to the last minute.

**2.** Always get the tricky stuff out of the way first. If you love practising the guitar but have a hard history report, do the history first and then practice, otherwise you'll get carried away doing the things you enjoy and forget all about work!

**3.** Turn off your phone and unless you need it to study, the internet.

**4.** If you need help, ask for it. Anyone teaching anything will always be happier knowing that you're clear about things.

**5.** Make sure you schedule lots of study breaks, especially if you're using a computer or researching in books. Your eyes can get tired really easily and once you're tired, you won't be able to do your best work.

**6.** Clear away any clutter around your study area. Too much mess can be distracting.

**7.** If it's a sunny day, try to study outside. The fresh air and change of scenery will help clear your head and you'll be able to concentrate for longer.

**8.** Make sure you reward yourself when your studying pays off. It'll make studying the next time seem so much more worth it.

# New projects

There are lots of ways to be inspired to start up a new project. Here are some of my favourites.

★ Always carry a notebook and a camera to write down your ideas and snap shots of anything interesting.

★ Read the newspaper or check the news online every day to see what's going on in the world.
★ Join a reading club. You could start one with your friends or sign up at the local library.

★ Research your favourite writer, singer or artist to find out how they got to where they are today and then create an inspiration board to hang in your study space.

★ Research the history of your street, village or town. Try interviewing an older family member, checking out the internet and the local library then write up your history and post it online.

★ Join an art class. If you don't think you'd be any good at painting, why not try sculpture? Or pottery?

★ Try and learn something new every day, whether it's one new word, the name of a flower in your garden or a chord on the guitar.

★ Every night, write down what you've seen, heard and learned in a journal. It'll help you keep track of all your thoughts and new projects.

Home

# Your room

It's important to make your space your own so that you have somewhere to get away from it all for some well-deserved me time! Here are some top tips on how to make your room feel special.

1. Tidying your room is a pain so try and put things away after you've used them. It sounds simple but it will make life a lot easier.

2. Put up lots of photographs of your friends and mementos of times you've had together. Pictures that remind you of fun and special times really personalise your room.

3. Once every couple of months, take out all of your clothes and make three piles. One to keep, one of things to go to the charity shop and one to recycle. It'll help you keep your cupboards tidy and remind you of fun outfits you had forgotten about. Check with your mama or papa before you get rid of anything though.

5. Your bed should be fit for a princess! Add lots of cushions and colourful throws to make it feel luxurious and try winding fairy lights around the headboard to make a fun reading light.

4. If you have the space, try and make separate areas in your room for different things. Keep the space around your bed clutter-free to help you relax. Keep your books and computer in one corner and go there when you need to concentrate. Your make-up, accessories and music can all go in another corner, dedicated to fun!

# Paint colours/fabrics

**One of the easiest ways to make your room feel more like home is to decorate it in your favourite colours. Try painting one big wall a bright colour or decorating your bed with some colourful throws. If you can't paint your room, make sure all your accessories match to make a bold statement.**

## White:
White is a very peaceful colour and is great at calming down energetic personalities. White bed linen is great if you're having trouble sleeping!

## Pink:
Pink might be your absolute favourite colour in the whole world but it can a little too energising on all four walls. If you really love pink, try putting it on the wall behind your bed so you can't see it when you're trying to sleep.

## Green:
Green is known as a harmonious colour that creates balance and calm so it's great in bedrooms. If you study or read in your bedroom, it's a great choice as green helps you think!

## Red:
Red creates a lot of energy and should only be used sparingly in a bedroom as it can stop you sleeping. Try putting a red throw on your bed so you can enjoy it in daytime but put it away at night.

## Yellow:
Yellow is cheerful and uplifting but, like pink, it can create lots of energy and make it difficult to calm down. Try it on a wall that gets a lot of natural light to echo the sunshine filling your room.

## Blue:
Blue is very restful and works well in bedrooms. Why not try painting your ceiling blue instead of white?

Remember, this will be the first colour you see in the morning and the last colour you see at night so make sure you love it!

# Get crafty

Wouldn't life be boring if everything was the same? One of the most fun ways to make your room truly yours, is to personalise some of your accessories.

Instead of buying a boring old swivel chair for your desk, pick up an old wooden dining chair from a charity shop or car boot sale. With a quick coat of paint and a new cushion, you've got a one-of-a-kind piece of furniture.

Instead of shoving things in storage boxes, look for old, rigid suitcases in second-hand shops. Aged leather ones are the best and look really cool. Tie little luggage tags to the handle to remind you what's inside. Perfect for storing your winter clothes!

To fancy up a lampshade, get a basic, pale fabric shade and doodle on a design with fabric pens.

# Get crafty

Instead of using boring drawing pins in your pin board, collect old badges or odd earrings and use them instead – much prettier!

If you have beautiful handbags or shoes that you love, don't hide them away in your cupboard. Dedicate a shelf to displaying them and make them a feature, plus, you won't forget to wear them.

Do you love your old T-shirt but know it's past its best? Well, pop a cushion pad inside the shirt and glue or stitch all the ends together to make a cool cushion!

Jazz up plain old photo frames with glitter glue. Just adding a touch here and there will help catch the light and make your pictures sparkle.

Cut-out your favourite images from magazines and make an inspiration board. Keep adding to it until it's full and then put it up on your wall to remind you of all the things that make you happy.

# The rules of being a good friend

Having friends is the best but remember, you have to be a good friend to keep good friends. I think a good friend should always:

★ Listen - don't just wait for your turn to speak!

★ Be honest.

35¢
SUNDAES

* Remember things that are important to your friends.
* Encourage each other to try new things together.
* Help each other out. Whether it's coaching your friend in a subject they're having trouble with or recording their favourite TV show when they're away.
* Keep secrets if your friend shares them with you. A good friend never gossips!

* Be there to make you smile. If your friend is feeling down, why not surprise them with a special note or their favourite cupcake to cheer them up.
* Never forget birthdays!
* Always support you. Even if everyone thinks you're crazy to take up rapping, a good friend will be there to cheer you on!

*Friends* 65

# How to show your friend you care

**It's really easy to forget to show friends how important they are. Try out some of these suggestions every so often and see how happy it makes them!**

★ If you take photos of things you've done together, always get two sets and give one to your friend.

★ Pack an extra cookie for them in your lunch.

★ Buy them a charm bracelet for their birthday and get a new charm every year, to celebrate important occasions or even just to show them you're thinking of them.

★ Start a friendship journal that only the two of you write in and make a scrapbook of all your adventures.

★ Help a friend with their chores. Everything seems easier when there are two of you.

★ Let them choose the movie the next time you visit the cinema.

★ Always send them a postcard from your holidays - not an email or a text!

SAFARI ADVENTURE

Get your friend a balloon for their birthday. Everyone loves balloons!

★ Send them a card or a note if they've done something they're proud off.
★ Arrange a fun night in with all your friend's favourite snacks and movies.

# Fun things to do with friends

 My favourite thing to do is to spend time with my friends. We have lots of fun together and we're always trying new things. Here are some of our favourite things to do!

At Christmas time, try a Secret Santa. Everyone puts their name in a hat and each person picks one of the friends. For a fun twist, why not agree to make each other's presents instead of buying them?

 Agree to learn something new together every month. Whether that means taking a dance class, listening to a language CD or just trying out a new cookie recipe, you'll never be bored!

Have a fashion swap party. Get all of your friends to bring along clothes and accessories they don't wear any more and then put on a fashion show for each other. At the end of the night, you can swap the things you don't want for cool new things.

Saturday Night Movie Club. Take it in turns to host a movie night each week. The host gets to choose one new and one classic movie and your friends bring the popcorn!

Pick a secret colour then all wear something that colour every day, even if it's just nail polish or a hairclip.

Go on a picnic to the park. Everyone brings one different thing to eat and afterwards, you can play games in the park.

What are your favourite things to do with your friends?

# What kind of friend are you?

Take this quiz and find out what kind of friend you are.

**1. Your best friend is feeling down and wants to hang out but you already have plans. What do you do?**

a) Invite lots of buddies to your house and hold a mini party for your friend. Music and dancing is sure to cheer them up.

b) Cancel your plans and invite your friend to your house. Your friend will feel better once they've talked everything out.

c) Go head with your plans but send your friend a text. There's no point you both being miserable.

d) Visit your friend armed with cookies and a big hug and then let them call the shots.

**2. You and your best friend have both fallen in love with the same pair of shoes! Her birthday is coming up and they would make the perfect present. Do you...**

a) Buy a pair for both of you. You can be shoes sisters!

b) Don't buy them at all. It wouldn't be fair for one of you to have them and not the other.

c) Buy the shoes for yourself. Your friend can always borrow them and she knows how shoe crazy you are.

d) Buy the shoes for your friend. She will be so touched that you remembered she liked them.

**3. You and your best friend want to see different movies at the cinema. What do you do?**

a) Toss a coin. Whoever wins gets to pick.

b) Let her pick, you don't want her to be disappointed.

c) Go and see your pick. You've wanted to see it for ages and she can always go to the other movie and meet you after.

d) See your movie this time, your friend picked last week, but make a date to see her movie next weekend.

**4. There is a big party next weekend but you're busy with your parents. Your best friend asks if she can borrow your new dress but you haven't worn it yet. Do you...**

a) Lend the dress to your friend. It should go to the party, even if you can't! You can't wait to see the pictures.

b) Lend the dress to your friend. You're not really a fan of big parties anyway.

c) Explain to your friend that you wanted to wear your dress that weekend.

d) Lend the dress to your friend and borrow her cool new boots in exchange. You love sharing with your buds, it's like having two wardrobes!

**5. Your friend wants to go horse riding for her birthday but you've never tried it before and are a little scared. What do you do?**

a) If everyone else is doing it, you'll go. You don't want to be left out.

b) Go along with your friends but decide not to ride the horses.

c) Suggest you do something else that you all enjoy like ice skating or going to a movie. There's no way you're getting on a horse!

d) Take a deep breath and get on that horse! How will you know whether or not you like it, if you don't try?

## Mostly c's

**You're a casual friend** You think it's more fun to have lots of different friends than one or two close friends. Everyone loves to have lots of buddies but try and spend a little more time getting to know your friends and then they'll be able to get to know you better too.

## Mostly d's

**You're the perfect pal** Everyone wants to be your friend. You know just when your friends want to hang out quietly and when they want to have fun and you'd never, ever forget anything as important as a birthday. Just remember to let your friends look after you, just as much as you look after them. Good friendship is about give and take.

## Mostly a's

**You're a fun friend** You are always encouraging your buddies to try new things. Everyone loves hanging out with you because you're so much fun to be around but don't forget, sometimes your friends might just want to hang out and relax. It's just as important to spend quality time listening and talking as it is having exciting adventures.

## Mostly b's

**You're a supportive friend** Your friends all turn to you when they need a shoulder to cry on. You're the perfect pal, who always listens and has the best advice but sometimes it might be fun to get out there and try something fun for a change. Challenge yourself to come up with one new idea a month to try out with a friend and see how much fun life can be!

Cooking

# Mama's apple pie

## Ingredients:

**For the pastry**
- ✴ 425g/15oz plain flour
- ✴ ½ tsp salt
- ✴ 100g/3½ oz caster sugar
- ✴ 250g/9oz butter, plus extra for greasing
- ✴ 1 free-range egg, beaten
- ✴ 2 free-range egg yolks

**For the filling**
- ✴ ½ orange, juice only
- ✴ 8 large cooking apples, peeled cored and cut into chunks
- ✴ 100g/3½ oz golden caster sugar
- ✴ 1 tbsp ground cinnamon

## Method

Mix the flour, salt, sugar and butter until the mixture resembles breadcrumbs. Slowly add the beaten egg and the egg yolks and combine until everything comes together. Once you have a dough, wrap it in clingfilm and place in the fridge to chill for half an hour.

**2.** Grease your pie dish and then heat the oven to 180°C/350°F/Gas mark 4. Always ask mama or papa to help you with the oven.

**3.** Once chilled, roll out two thirds of the pastry until it is twice as wide as the cake tin. Lift it up carefully and lay it over the cake tin, pressing it gently into the bottom and the sides.

**4.** Carefully line the pastry with a sheet of baking paper and fill it with baking beans. Bake in the oven for 12-15 minutes, or until the pastry is pale golden-brown. Remove from the oven, take out the baking beans and baking paper and leave the pastry to cool a little. You can turn the oven temperature down to 170°C/325°F/Gas mark 3.

**5.** Chop your apples into chunks, sprinkle them with sugar and pour on the orange juice. Now place the apples into the pastry case.

**6.** Roll out the rest of the pastry until it is large enough to cover the cake tin. Brush the edge of the pastry case with a little bit of beaten egg and place the lid on top of the pie. Seal the pastry to the case by pinching the edges together and trim off any excess.

**7.** Make two small holes in the centre of the pastry lid to allow steam to escape while your pie is cooking away. Brush the pastry lid with a little beaten egg mixture. Now bake for 35-40 mins, or until golden-brown.

# Chocolate chip cookies

## Ingredients

* 350g/12½ oz flour
* 1 tsp baking soda
* 1 tsp ground ginger
* 225g/8oz butter
* 175g/6½ oz golden caster sugar
* 175g/6½ oz soft brown sugar
* 1 tsp vanilla extract
* 2 eggs
* 350g/12½ oz white and milk chocolate chunks

## Method

1. Ask a grown-up to preheat the oven to 190°C/375°F/Gas mark 5.

2. Mix the flour, baking soda and ginger together in a bowl then throw in your chocolate chunks.

**3.** Cream together the butter, sugar, brown sugar and vanilla extract until creamy in another bowl and then beat in the eggs.

**4.** Using your hands, mix the dry ingredients into the wet mixture and knead until you have a dough.

**5.** Pull the dough into small balls, about the size of a golf ball. Place on a greased baking sheet and flatten slightly with a fork. Make sure there is plenty of space around each cookie.

**6.** Bake for about ten minutes or until the cookies are golden brown.

# Fruit smoothies

## Basic smoothie ingredients:

★ 1 banana
★ ½ pot of fat-free natural yoghurt
★ 2 teaspoons of clear honey

Blend all the ingredients together with some ice cubes for a quick and delicious fruity treat!

**Pineapple and blueberry:**
Add two handfuls of pineapple chunks and a handful of blueberries for a refreshing berry blast.

**Banana and peanut butter:**
replace the honey with a couple of tablespoons of peanut butter and a teaspoon of maple syrup.

**Kiwi and raspberry:** Add one sliced kiwi and a handful of raspberries to the banana mix for a tropical smoothie twist.

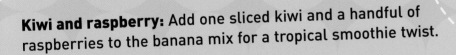

# Picnic recipes

Picnic treats needs to be easy to carry and easy to eat!
Try some of these delicious treats at your next picnic.
Always ask Mama or Papa to help with the oven.

## Mini Brownies

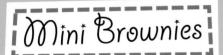

### Ingredients
* 100g/3.5oz dark chocolate
* 150g/5.3oz butter
* 125g/4.4oz plain flour
* 400g/14.1oz golden caster sugar
* 3 eggs
* 120g/4.2oz chopped nuts
* 1 teaspoon vanilla extract

### Method
1. Ask a grown-up helper to pre-heat the oven to 180°C/350°F/Gas Mark 4.
2. Break up your chocolate and cut the butter into cubes and melt in the microwave on low for about a minute. Keep an eye on this as the chocolate and butter can melt very quickly. Once melted, stir together.
3. Beat the eggs together in a separate bowl.
4. Slowly stir in the sugar, the vanilla extract, then the eggs, the flour and finally nuts and combine.
5. Pour the mixture into a 30 x 23cm/12 x 9 inch greased baking tin and smooth down then pop carefully in the oven.
6. Bake for about thirty minutes or until a skewer comes out of the centre almost clean.
7. Leave to cool, then cut into small squares and wrap in foil to take on your picnic!

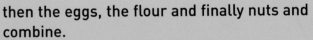

## Banana Tea Bread

### Ingredients
* 225g/7.9oz plain flour
* 1 tblsp baking powder
* 150g/5.3oz light golden caster sugar
* 100g/3.5oz light cream cheese
* 2 eggs (beaten)
* 180g/6.3oz mashed bananas
* 50ml brewed tea

### Method
1. Ask a grown-up helper to pre-heat the oven to 180°C/350°F/Gas Mark 4.
2. Mix together the flour and baking powder in one bowl and in another, cream together the sugar, cream cheese and eggs until they are fluffy. Then mix in the mashed bananas and tea.
3. Combine the two mixtures and mix until smooth.
4. Pour the cake batter into a 23 x 12cm/9 x 5 inch greased loaf tin and place carefully into the oven for around 60 minutes or until a skewer comes out of the centre completely clean.
5. Let the loaf cool on a wire rack then turn out from the tin and cut into slices for your picnic.

## Easy Pizza

### Ingredients
* 2 x ready made pizza bases
* 1 jar passata
* 1 pack mozzarella cheese
* Your favourite toppings

1. Spread two tablespoons of passata over the top of the pizza base.
2. Carefully slice the mozzarella into thin slices and lay over the passata. Now add your favourite toppings.
3. Top with another couple of slices of mozzarella - this will help hold all the toppings onto your pizza when it is cold.
4. Cook according to the instructions on the pizza base packs then leave to cool.
5. Once cold, you can pack for your picnic.

Hobbies

# Sports

**There are lots of fun sports to try.
Here are a few of my favourites!**

## Basketball...

Is lots of fun! All you need is a ball and
a hoop and you've got yourself a game.
You can even practice on your own.

## Tennis...

Is my favourite sport to play
in the summer. Who doesn't
look cute in tennis whites?

## Baseball...

Is the perfect post-picnic pick me up. Just remember to take a bat, a ball and lots of friends.

## Football...

Is the most popular game in London, where I live. Just grab a ball and some friends and start scoring!

# Music

I love music and would like to learn to play lots of different instruments.

At the moment I'm learning the guitar - would you like to learn too? If you learn these three chords, you'll be able to make up a song!

x o      o x    o      o x x o

**A major**

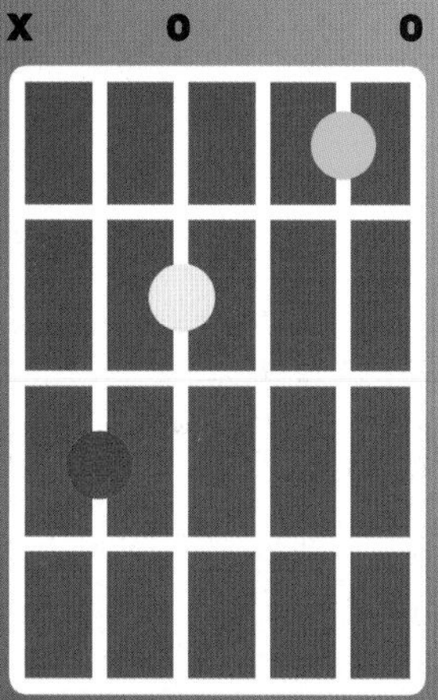

**C major**

**D major**

Start practising by making up set lists of your favourite songs and then seeing how well they sound together. If your set makes you want to dance, then it's a winner!

If you don't want to learn an instrument, how about being a DJ? DJs play records to people but it takes a long time to learn to do it well.

# Writing poetry

Writing poetry doesn't have to be hard. Try writing down exactly what you're feeling or what you can see out of your window.

Haikus are special kinds of Japanese poems that have seventeen syllables, split over three lines like this:

London is my home
It is a very big place
For Hello Kitty

I love apple pie
Hot from the oven with cream
It is delicious

Some friends live nearby
Some friends live too far away
But friends are the best

Your poems can be about anything, the only rule is that they have five syllables in the first line, seven in the second and five in the last line. Why don't you give it a try?

# Dancing

Dancing is the best! I like to dance with my friends all the time. We love to listen to our favourite music and make up routines.

 We also like to learn different kinds of dances. Some of my favourites are...

*Tap*

*Ballet*

Disco

What's your favourite
kind of dancing?

# Goodbye!

I hope you've had fun reading my book. There are so many great things to do, sometimes I think I won't have time to do them all! It can be tough deciding what to do first but I usually end up baking the mini brownies to help me choose...

Why don't you start right now by picking one thing and then starting a journal to record what you get up to. One day, it could become your very own guide to life!

Lots of love,

*Hello Kitty* xx